The Voice of the Wood

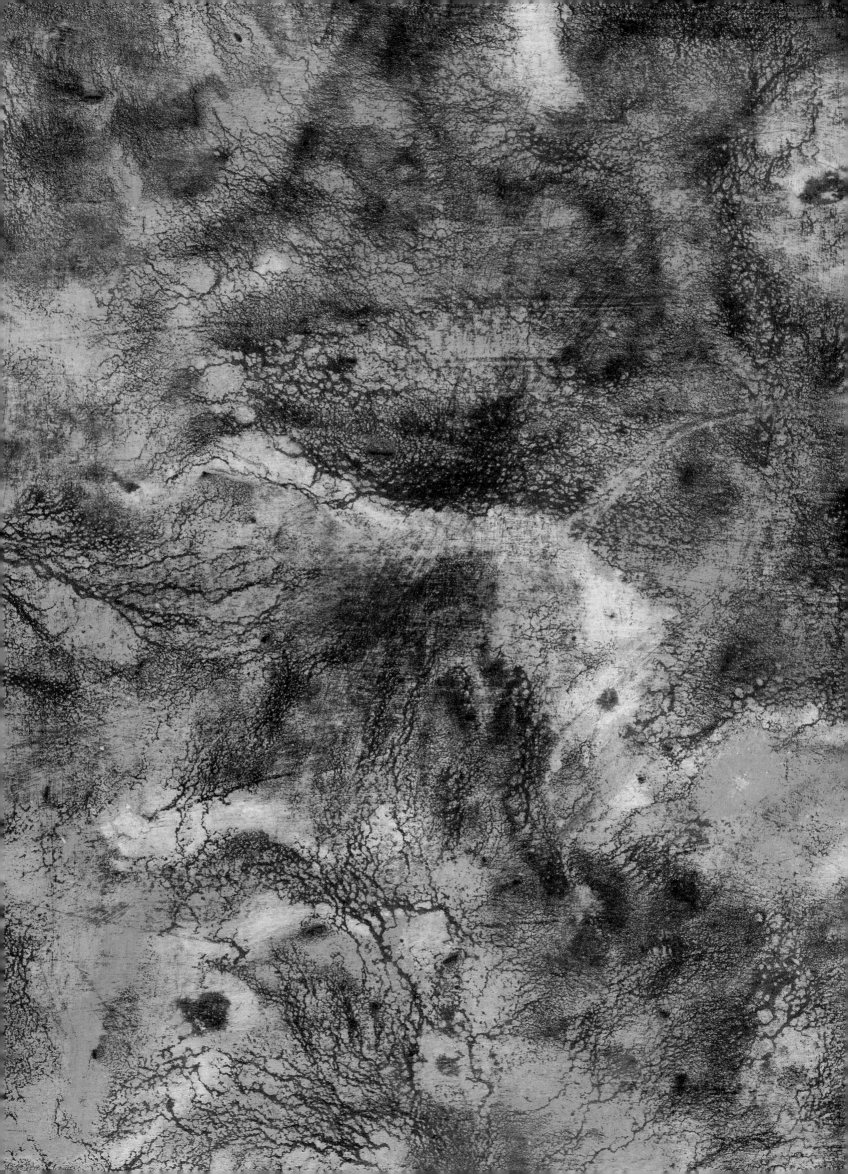

The Voice of the Wood

Claude Clément · paintings by Frédéric Clément

translation by Lenny Hort

A Puffin Pied Piper

Long ago in Venice, where the streets and highways are canals,
a craftsman lived over the studio in which he made fine musical
instruments. The front of his house overlooked a busy canal,
but the back opened into a peaceful little garden. Spreading its
leafy branches out over the garden, there was a great old tree.

The craftsman loved that tree. As he rested in its shade or gazed out the window into its branches, he could hear a symphony of birds singing, leaves swaying, and boats gliding by. No violin in his shop, no concert in Venice, could match the beauty of that music.

But one hard winter the old tree died. When spring came,
no buds sprouted, no leaves rustled, no birds came to nest.

Sadly, the craftsman had the old tree chopped down, stripped of its bark and branches, and cut into lumber. The wood was stowed away in a corner of his attic, and he went back to his work.

The years passed. Tides rose and fell under the bridges of Venice. The craftsman's hair began to turn gray. He seldom ventured out of his studio, but the world's best musicians flocked to him to buy violins and cellos.

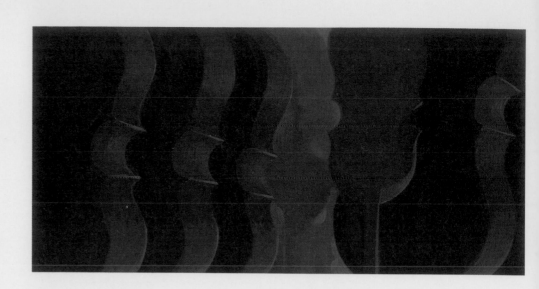

One day the old man came across the wood from his beloved tree. He thought back fondly of that tree and its strange, beautiful music. Running his fingers over the wood, the old craftsman knew what he must do. He would take that wood and build his masterpiece, a cello as much in tune with the music of nature as his old friend the tree had been. Day after day, season after season, he worked, polishing and shaping the wood. A year passed and then, on the day of the Grand Carnival, the cello was finished.

All the streets and canals bustled with men and women in fabulous costumes. Magicians, clowns, and musicians filled every square. The old craftsman looked up from his masterpiece and gazed out at the merriment. "Is there anyone in that noisy crowd," he said, "who can possibly make my cello sing?"

As he spoke, a young man pressed through the crowd. He wore a wig and costume, and his face was painted and masked, but everyone he passed recognized him as a famous musician. A group of his friends followed him into the craftsman's studio.

The musician looked admiringly at the cello, but when he reached toward it the craftsman warned him. "This is a magical cello. Only the most gifted fingers, and only a heart in tune with the voice of the wood, can play it." The young man was furious. He snatched the cello and tried to play. But the instrument seemed to have a spirit of its own. What poured out was not a sweet melody like a nightingale, but brutal, grating noises, like crocodiles chewing and clawing their way across the floor.

The musician kept on trying until his friends could stand no more
and stole away. The craftsman shrugged and went up to bed.
The musician tore off his wig in despair. He hurled his mask
and costume to the floor and wiped the paint off his face. And
then, exhausted, humiliated, and alone, he picked up the cello
and held it as if he had never played before.

In the morning the old craftsman awoke to the loveliest, most magical music he had ever heard. He looked out into the garden and there he saw the young man playing the cello. Leafy branches had sprouted from the cello's neck and swayed mysteriously in the breeze. As the old man gazed, a flock of songbirds landed and added their own music to the voice of the wood.

PUFFIN PIED PIPER BOOKS
Published by the Penguin Group
Penguin Books USA Inc., 375 Hudson Street, New York, New York 10014, U.S.A.
Penguin Books Ltd, 27 Wrights Lane, London W8 5TZ, England
Penguin Books Australia Ltd, Ringwood, Victoria, Australia
Penguin Books Canada Ltd, 10 Alcorn Avenue, Toronto, Ontario, Canada M4V 3B2
Penguin Books (N.Z.) Ltd, 182-190 Wairau Road, Auckland 10, New Zealand
Penguin Books Ltd, Registered Offices: Harmondsworth, Middlesex, England
First published in hardcover in the United States 1989 by Dial Books
A Division of Penguin Books USA Inc.

Published in Belgium 1988 by Pastel,
an imprint of l'école des loisirs, as *Le Luthier de Venise*
Copyright © 1988 by l'école des loisirs, Paris
American text copyright © 1989 by Dial Books
Translated by Lenny Hort
All rights reserved
Typography by Amelia Lau Carling
Library of Congress Catalog Card Number: 88-22892
Printed in Hong Kong
First Puffin Pied Piper Printing 1993
ISBN 0-14-054594-8
10 9 8 7 6 5 4 3 2 1

A Pied Piper Book is a registered trademark of Dial Books,
a division of Penguin Books USA Inc.,
® TM 1,163,686 and ® TM 1,054,312.

THE VOICE OF THE WOOD
is also available in hardcover from Dial Books.

The art for each picture consists of an acrylic
painting, which is color-separated and reproduced
in blue, red, yellow, and black halftones.

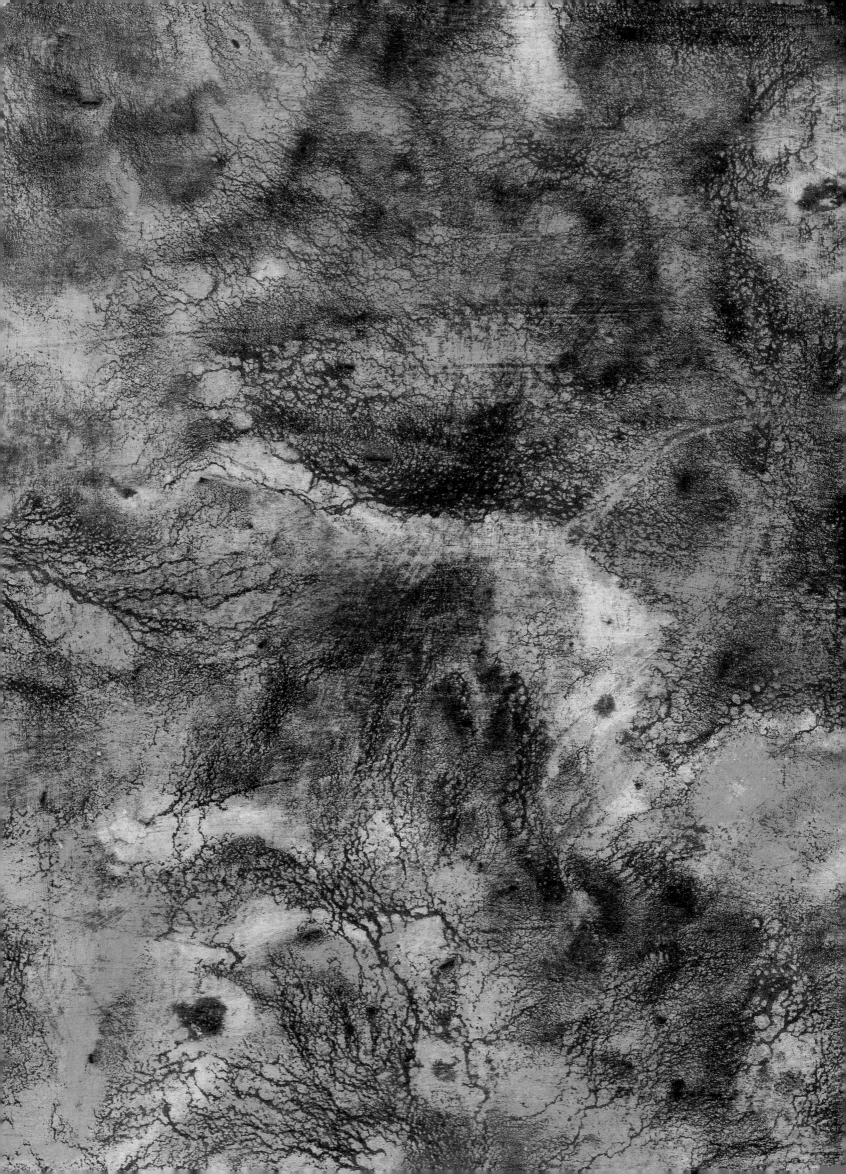

Claude Clément

is the author of many books for children, including *The Painter and the Wild Swans* (Dial), which received the French Foundation Grand Prize for Children's Literature. Ms. Clément has three children and lives in Paris.

Frédéric Clément

is an award-winning illustrator whose pictures have appeared in more than twenty books, including *The Painter and the Wild Swans* by Claude Clément. Also a painter and designer, Mr. Clément received the International Grand Prize at Bratislava and the European Children's Literature Prize. Mr. Clément lives in France. Although he and Claude Clément have the same surname, they are not related.